The Pearl in the Grass

A story from China

Retold by **John Harris**

Illustrated by **Tom Morgan-Jones**

notreallybooks….. really good stories

The Pearl in the Grass

First published 2009 by notreallybooks
Suite 111, Dorset House, Duke Street, Chelmsford CM1 1TB.

Text copyright John Harris 2008
Illustrations copyright Tom Morgan-Jones 2008

The rights of John Harris and Tom Morgan-Jones to be
identified as author and illustrator respectively of this work have
been asserted by them in accordance with the Copyright, Designs
and Patents Act 1988

ISBN 978-0-9552129-3-2

A catalogue record for this book is available from the
British Library

Printed in Lavenham, Suffolk, by the Lavenham Press

notreallybooks.biz

johnharristhestoryteller.com

Thanks to Nat Scurll, Bill Byford, Andrea, Fran and Tom.

The Pearl in the Grass

A story from China

Retold by **John Harris**

Illustrated by **Tom Morgan-Jones**

Suite 111, Dorset House, 25 Duke Street, Chelmsford CM1 1TB

wwwnotreallybooks.biz

To the thousands of children
all over the country
who've taken a deep breath
and spread their arms
as I've reached the end of this story.....

this book's for you.

One – Xiang and Sheng, a widow and her son

A long, long time ago there was a village by a river in the middle of China.

The people of the village never wandered very far and never really had to: with the water from the river they could drink as much as they liked, water their gardens, grow their food and feed their animals. They could wash their clothes as well as themselves, and even swim and have fun when their work was done.

Towards the east, about five miles from the village, was a very big lake. The water was cool and blue and full of the most amazing fish. Around the lake there were thick, dark forests with all kinds of wild animals, and tall and graceful mountains which had snow on the top for most of the year. But no-one from the village liked to go near the lake, because high in the mountains there were caves, and in the caves there lived a band of robbers. These robbers were really nasty people who would rob anyone who came near their mountain. Rich people, poor people, frail, elderly people, no-one was safe from the robbers because they didn't just rob for a living, they did it for fun too. So the people of the village stayed close to their homes, and close to the river that looked after them so well.

In this village there lived a widow called Xiang, who had a young son called Sheng.

Xiang and Sheng were, without doubt, the poorest people in the village.

They were the poorest people for miles around.

They were the poorest people in the county.

They might well have been the poorest people in the whole of China.

They were the only people in the village who didn't have animals in their garden.

Not as pets, you understand, but for food.

Everyone else had animals in their gardens.

Even the other poor people had a couple of hens so they could have eggs for breakfast, and better off people had goats and pigs and all sorts.

But not Sheng and his mum. They couldn't afford anything like that.

They were so poor that Sheng couldn't go to school. The children had to pay the teacher every morning for that day's lessons, and Xiang hardly ever had enough money. So while his friends went to school and learned to read and write and count, Sheng had to go to work.

And the work was hard.

Every day he had to walk away from the village, to the land that no-one actually owned, where the wild grass grew tall and straight. Using a long, sharp knife he had to cut down as much of the wild grass as he could carry. Then he had to tie the grass up into little

bundles, tie the little bundles into one great big bundle, put the big bundle onto his back and carry it all the way back to the village.

Every day there was a market in the village square and Sheng sold the grass at the market. Everyone else in the village had animals, and they bought Sheng's grass to feed them with.

The other villagers could just as easily have gone for a walk and taken the grass themselves for free, but if they bought it from Sheng it meant they had one less job to do and that would save them time and trouble.

And besides, everyone liked Sheng. They knew how poor he and Xiang were and felt sorry for them, so they bought Sheng's grass.

One way or another Sheng and Xiang got by.

They never had much, but they always had each other.

But when Sheng was about ten years old something strange happened:

it didn't rain in the spring.

Now we all know that it has to rain in the spring: in the autumn and the winter everything falls back and goes to sleep and then, in the spring, everything starts to wake up and grow back again, and needs the water to grow back properly.

But it didn't rain.

Not a drop.

Not a

single

tiny

precious

drop.

Anywhere.

Well, not quite anywhere: some travellers coming through the village told them that it had rained in the north of the country, but for miles and miles around Sheng's village the ground was hard and dry.

After the long winter Sheng and his mum had very little food or money left so it was important that he found fresh grass to cut and sell.

Every day he had to walk further and further before he found the kind of grass that people would pay for, and when he did find some there wasn't very much.

It seemed to him as if the whole world was drying up and all the grass was dying.

The strange, dry, spring turned into a hot, dry summer. All day every day the sky was a rich deep blue without a cloud in sight. The sun seemed to rise quickly every morning and from high in the sky it would stare down at the world like an angry God burning everything dry.

The ground was hard and dry.

The grass was turning to straw then falling into dust.

The crops weren't growing properly and - worst of all - the river was beginning to dry up.

Every day Sheng walked further and further in the blistering heat looking for grass. It seemed to him as if the whole world was turning into desert. Every day he had to walk so far before he found anything to sell that he only just got back to the village before the market closed. Every day he brought back less grass and brought home less money than the day before. At this rate he knew there would soon be no grass left anywhere. If it didn't start raining soon they didn't know what they were going to do.

There was still food for sale in the market, but people were bringing it down from the north, where it had rained as usual and there was plenty of food growing. But because it was coming from so far away it was very expensive. No-one in the village could afford very much of it, and poor Xiang could hardly afford anything at all.

One evening Xiang and Sheng were sitting at the kitchen table, sharing a bowl of rice for supper. Xiang took a deep breath and said "Listen, son, I've got something to tell you: I think it would be best if you

left home and went to live up in the north."

"Why?" he asked.

"Because I don't think things are going to get any better here," she said. "There's no sign of rain and hardly any food in the village. The river's almost dry. This is what's called a drought, when there isn't any water. And a drought leads to a famine, where there isn't any food. And when there's no food people die."

"Then you'll have to come with me," he said.

"No, it's better if you go on your own.

"Why?"

"Because you're a clever boy and you're hard working," she said. "Someone will give you a job and somewhere to live. But if I go with you I'll slow you down along the way, and when you get to wherever you're going you'll have to find somewhere big enough for me to live as well. I won't find a job. I don't have any skills, there's really not very much I can do, so I'll just slow you down on the way and be a burden to you when you get there. You're better off without me."

"No I'm not!" he said.

"Yes you are," she replied.

"But if you stay here you'll die," he said. "You've just said so yourself."

"Oh, don't worry about me," she said. "I'll manage."

"No you won't! You have to come with me," he said. But Xiang shook her head slowly, and Sheng could see she meant it. He didn't want to leave his home, and he didn't want to leave his mum, but he began to think she might be right. He might have to.

But he knew he couldn't leave her, whatever happened.

"I'll tell you what," he said. "I'll pack a bag and go up north tomorrow, like you said. But as soon as I find something we can eat, or something we can sell to buy food with, I'll bring it straight home. I won't leave you. I won't let you down."

'You're a brave, sweet and kind boy," she said, "and you've always taken care of me," and she kissed him on the head. "If you do find something to eat or sell then that would be wonderful," she said. "But I mean it: if you can't, then you must go up to the north and stay there. I won't mind, I want you to look after yourself."

Sheng kissed his mum and went to bed without being told to. He knew he'd need his sleep for the long journey he'd have the next day. He was determined to take care of them both.

Two – a long journey

In the morning he wrapped a blanket around his knife and stuffed it into his bag along with a small amount of cooked rice. A bottle of precious river water hung from his belt.

He kissed his mum goodbye and set off along the north road.

He walked all day without stopping.

The sun was high, the sky was blue, and very soon he was hot, sticky, sweaty and tired.

But he kept on going, marching steadily towards the north.

And all day he didn't see another living creature.

Not a bird in the sky, not a person on the road.

He did see a couple of animals lying beside the road, but they'd died from thirst some time ago. Sheng felt sorry for the animals, and a little afraid for himself. If they couldn't survive, what chance did he have?

At the end of the day, when it was too dark for him to go any further, he curled up in a ditch by the side of the road and slept completely covered by the blanket. He had to hide under the blanket because he knew that at night some of the robbers would come along the road on horseback, looking for people who'd foolishly stayed out too late. If they found a small boy

on the road on his own, with nothing worth stealing, they'd probably take him back to the mountains to work for them.

He slept very lightly that night, waking up at the slightest sound. More than once he heard the sound of horses cantering along the road and once or twice they actually slowed down as they rode past him. He hardly dared breath in case the robbers heard anything and became suspicious. He stayed absolutely still, breathing slowly, listening carefully, not daring to lift his head from under the blanket, until - at last - they rode off into the night.

In the morning he had a little rice for breakfast, packed his bag again and set off, marching further along the road through the heat and dust.

His feet were getting sore and the straps of his bag were rubbing against his shoulders. The heat made him sweat so much he wasn't sure if his clothes were sticking to him or he was sticking to his clothes.

Later in the morning he realized he had company: a vulture was flying high above, circling the air as it followed him. Sheng knew that vultures don't actually kill things, they look for something they think is going to die, wait until it does die and then eat it. Since Sheng was probably the only living creature the vulture could see, even from that great height, it was pretty obvious what the bird was thinking.

"Go away!' he shouted, but the vulture ignored him. An hour later it was still there, circling overhead.

"Get lost!" he shouted again.

The vulture squawked back at him. It was a rough and threatening noise which probably meant "Don't be silly - I'm starving!"

An hour later it was still there.

"Please.... go away!" Sheng cried. It squawked again, but didn't go.

Then he had an idea. Gradually he slowed down almost to a standstill, as if he was suddenly so tired he could hardly go on. Then he stumbled down onto his hands and knees. He knew he was being watched with interest as he slowly crawled a few more yards along the road, but from that height the vulture wouldn't see him picking up small stones as he did so.

Finally he rolled flat onto his back with his arms and legs spread wide, staring lifelessly up into the sky, looking for all the world as if he was dead.

'And about time, too!' the vulture thought, and flew down to have his breakfast.

But as it flew closer towards the body Sheng suddenly came back to life and the bird was pelted with stones. The bird flew off with an angry squawk and Sheng watched as it gradually became just a dot that was so far away he wasn't even sure if he could really see it.

The vulture turned out to be the only living thing Sheng saw on his journey, and by the end of the day he was almost missing the company.

Three – something in the distance

It was in the afternoon of the third day that he suddenly noticed something so strange he thought he was imagining things. He stopped and looked carefully to make sure his eyes weren't playing tricks with him.

Way off in the distance, about half a mile from where he was, there seemed to be a patch of green in the middle of all the baked, dry, dead ground.

"That's grass," he said to himself, but then he told himself it couldn't be. How could a patch of grass be growing in the middle of nothing? Everything else for miles around was dead. All he could see in any direction was desert. How could grass be growing there when nothing else was?

He thought he'd better go and take a look, though, just to be sure.

It took him a while to reach it and when he did he could hardly believe his eyes: It was a patch of grass! A beautiful, rich, lush, dark green patch of grass about twice as tall as he was, growing in the middle of nothing. He couldn't understand it: there was no water anywhere in sight, no stream or spring or river, and the ground was as dry and dead and dusty as everything else for miles around.

There was no reason why this grass should be there.

It simply shouldn't have been growing where it was. But it was. Big and tall and green and staring him in the face.

"How can you be growing here?" he laughed as he asked the grass out loud. Of course he didn't get an answer - he'd have been shocked if he did - but he realized it really didn't matter how or why. What mattered was that it was good quality grass and he'd get a good price for it at the market.

He dropped his bag onto the ground, took out his knife and with swift, bold strokes cut as much of the grass as he could possibly carry. He tied lengths of the grass into knots, then tied the knots into a great big bundle and swung the bundle up and round and on to his back.

"Whoah!" he cried out as it swung round and almost knocked him over. It was heavier than he'd expected. He stood still for a moment, getting his breath and balance back and adjusting the load so it was a little more comfortable. Then he took a deep breath, leaned forward slightly and set off for home.

Carrying it back along the dry and dusty road was very hard work. He had hardly any rice left and was weak with hunger. Sometimes he stumbled and fell over, grazing his knees and hands, and often he had no choice but to stop and rest.

It took him five days to carry it back along the road and when he got back to the village he was hot,

sweaty,

hungry,

thirsty,

very very homesick

and very, very, very tired.

But he didn't go straight home. He staggered to the market place, swung the bundle round and off his back and fell onto it himself as it landed in a corner of the square. He got his breath back and then straightened up and stood beside it.

"Grass!" he called out rather weakly, "I've got grass! Fresh grass for sale! Anybody want any fresh grass?"

Once he'd attracted their attention the people of the village were amazed. "Hey look!" people called out to each other. "Sheng's got grass!" Other people came over to see for themselves. "Good stuff as well!" someone else said, and everyone agreed. They'd not seen grass as good as this for as long as they could remember.

"Well done, son!"

"Where did you find this?"

"How much do you want for it? I'll have some!"

"Me too!"

"And me, please, Sheng!"

In no time at all he'd sold it all for a good price, making more money in a few minutes than he'd ever made in a week before.

When he got home his mum was thrilled to see him. He'd been away for so long she thought he'd decided to stay in the north after all and she didn't think she'd ever see him again. She hugged and kissed him and cried with joy, and it was ages before she finally let go of him and he got the chance to empty his pockets.

When she saw how much money he'd made she jumped up and down, whooping with delight, squeezing his cheeks and telling him what a clever boy he was. She scooped it all up and took it back to the market, where she bought all the food that he loved to eat which they couldn't afford before.

That night she cooked him the most wonderful supper he'd ever had, with everything he loved to eat chopped up and stir fried and served with rice and noodles and loads of fresh juicy fruit to end the meal.

When he'd eaten everything she'd placed before him he sat back in his chair feeling fuller and more satisfied than he'd ever felt in his life. "Thanks, mum, that was wonderful!" he sighed. He really couldn't remember the last time he'd eaten so well or felt so full. But you know how it is sometimes when you eat a big meal: it makes you feel so relaxed the next thing you know you're feeling sleepy. Sheng suddenly realized how utterly exhausted he was.

He yawned loudly and hardly had the strength to say "I'm sorry Mum, I'm really tired and I'm going to have to go to bed now!" He kissed her goodnight and staggered sleepily towards his bedroom. His bed was just a thin mattress on the floor but when he opened the door he was so pleased to see his bed that he fell straight down on top of it without even taking his clothes off and was fast asleep right away.

He slept all night.

He slept all night and all the next day.

And all the next night as well.

He missed out a whole day of his life by sleeping right through it.

"Morning, sleepyhead!" his mum said as he walked groggily into the kitchen, "and where were you yesterday?"

"Bringing the grass back," he said as he slumped down onto a chair.

"That was the day before!" she laughed.

"Uh?"

"You slept right through yesterday! You must have been tired, you poor thing. Are you ready for some breakfast?"

"Oh yes, please!" he said. He was hungry again after such a long sleep.

"You sit down and it'll be ready in a minute."

And it was! There was fruit to begin with and a sort of porridge and then there were scrambled eggs and freshly baked bread and all kinds of things he'd never eaten before but which all tasted wonderful, and fruit juice and green tea to drink.

He ran his finger over his plate to scrape up the last bit of scrambled egg while his mum wasn't looking, pushed his chair back to make a bit more room for his swollen tummy and stretched his legs out. "Thanks, Mum, that was wonderful."

"Don't get too comfy", his mum said as she cleared away the bowls, "you've got to pack your bag soon."

"Where are we going?" he asked.

"I'm staying here," she said, "but you're going off to get more grass, aren't you" she asked.

"What?????" his heart sank at the thought of going all that way again.

She was surprised that he was so surprised. "Why not?" she asked. "You said yourself you only brought back some of the grass, but look how much money you made! It makes sense for you to go back there as soon as you can and bring back some more!"

"I suppose so," he sighed.

At least this time he had good food to take with him for the journey. After breakfast he had a wash and got dressed, packed his bag with his knife and his blanket and then crammed so much food into it that it was bulging at the seams, kissed his mum goodbye and set off.

Four - there and back again

Again it took Sheng three days to get back to where the grass was growing.

Three days long walk.

Three days of heat and dust.

Three days of thirst - he had plenty of food this time but water was still scarce.

Three days in which he didn't see another living creature.

Not even a vulture.

Three days in which he could easily believe he was the only thing left alive in the world.

And when he got back to where the grass grew he stood and stared in amazement: the grass he'd cut down had already grown back up to the same height as the rest. There was just as much for him to cut down as there had been before. He had the strangest feeling it had been waiting for him to come back.

He'd only been to school for two or three days in his whole life, so he wasn't the world's best mathematician. But he could just about work this out:

When he found this grass it had taken him five days to get home.

(He counted out the fingers on one hand.)

Then he was at home for two nights.

(He held out two more.)

Then it took him another three days to get back here.

(He was running out of fingers.)

Which meant this grass had grown back to the same height after just.....

(he counted all his fingers again to make sure)

.....ten days!

"Ten days????" He found himself talking out loud to the grass again. "How can you grow back so high in just ten days?" As if in reply a gentle breeze blew through the grass which seemed to make it whisper, though Sheng couldn't tell what it said. He didn't understand how grass could grow so quickly, but then again it didn't really matter. What mattered was that it had grown back and so all he had to do was cut the same amount down again and take it home again, which is exactly what he did.

Once again it took him five days to get back to the village.

Five difficult, long and hot days.

Five days with a heavy load on his back.

Five days of bare, dried, cracked earth under his feet and the sun in his eyes all day.

When he reached the village square it took him minutes to sell all the grass and once again he had a pile of money to take home to his mum. Again she kissed and hugged him, squeezed his cheeks, told him what a clever boy he was, and, after popping back to the market for the food, cooked him a wonderful supper.

By the time he'd finished eating he was so tired he could barely keep his eyes open. His mum was so happy and excited to see him again that she would probably have chatted away all night, but he was so exhausted he could hardly make sense of what she was saying. He felt bad about leaving her up while he went to bed but he knew he had to. He kissed her goodnight and staggered towards his bedroom. He smiled with relief when he saw his mattress, fell straight down onto it still with his clothes on and was fast asleep.

You won't be at all surprised to hear that he slept right through the night, all through the next day and all through the next night.

When he did wake up his mum made him the same delicious breakfast as before. He was still feeling quite tired as she cleared away the bowls. "I suppose now I have to go back to get more grass?" he sighed.

"Yes, but I've had an idea," she smiled and sat down opposite him. "This time you need to take a spade and a sack."

"Why?" he asked.

"Well think about it," she said. "If the grass grows back that quickly there's no need for you to be trekking backwards and forwards all the time, cutting it down, packing it up and bringing it all the way home again."

"What else can I do?"

"We can grow it in our garden!"

"How can we do that?" he asked.

"If you take a spade and a sack you can dig up -" she held her arms apart "about this much of the ground it's growing in so we get the roots as well. Bring it home in the sack and we can plant it in the garden!"

"Won't work," he said, but she didn't seem to hear him.

"If it grows that quickly we'll be able to sell some every few days. That way you won't have to go all that way, sleeping rough and dodging the robbers, and I won't have to worry about you: you'll be safe at home with me and we'll have a nice steady income from selling some of the grass every day or so!"

"It's ridiculous," he said.

"What's ridiculous?"

"Growing the grass here!'

"What's ridiculous about growing the grass here? It makes sense!"

"No it doesn't. It won't work."

"Why not?" she asked.

"Haven't you forgotten something?" he asked.

"What?"

"It hasn't rained here for nearly a year! The garden's like a desert - how are we going to grow grass in it?"

"A-ha!" she smiled as she held a hand up to stop him. "I've been awake most of the night thinking about this. Just because it hasn't rained doesn't meant we can't water the garden!"

"The river's dried up," he reminded her.

"Ah, yes, but the lake hasn't!" She was looking so excited he began to worry that she'd lost her mind. "While you're away getting the grass I'll get all the water we need for the garden from the lake!"

"What?" he could hardly believe his ears.

"I'll get water from the lake!" she was almost laughing with excitement. "I'll borrow a bucket," (they were so poor they didn't actually own a bucket themselves) "and I'll get water from the lake!"

"Mum, it's five miles to the lake! That means you're going to be walking five miles each way - ten miles in total - just for one bucket of water!"

"All right - I'll borrow two buckets!" she laughed, "that'll make it twice as easy!"

"That's still ten miles for two buckets of water," he said. "You can't keep walking backwards and forwards for ten miles at a time. It's a silly idea and it'll never work."

"Yes it will!" she said again. "You should have more faith!"

"It won't work," he tried to sound calm and reasonable. "It's too far. You'll exhaust yourself. In this heat you'll probably kill yourself! It's too much, and it's not even safe: what about the robbers?"

But her mind was made up and she would not be put off the idea. The more he tried to persuade her the more she gave him that look that mums all over the world give their children when they've had enough of arguing with them, and Sheng knew he had to go along with the idea, however stupid it might seem. "All right," he sighed as he gave in, "we'll give it a try."

So off he set again, with his bag full of food and a sack and a spade as well as his knife and blanket. Sure enough when he got to the grass three days later it had grown back to the same height again. This certainly was the strangest grass he'd ever come across.

It took a huge effort to get the spade into the hard, dry ground. As he began to work some of the ground loose so that he could get the spade out again something strange happened. A gentle breeze blew through the grass, but this time the sound it made was less like a whisper and more like a moan. Suddenly there were goosebumps on his arms and a shiver ran down his spine. He told himself he was being silly and carried on.

He lifted the spade and with a huge effort sank it into the ground again and this time the grass seemed to cry out with pain. He stopped and looked all around him to make sure he was alone. There was silence all around him, and absolute stillness. The only movement he could detect was off towards the horizon where the heat coming up from the ground made things appear to wobble, and he knew that was just an illusion.

He turned back to his work, but every time he sank the spade into the ground a breeze would blow through the grass. He knew he was just imagining it, but it seemed as if the grass was warning him not to dig, and as he ignored it the sound turned more to one of anger. He knew he was being silly but he couldn't help feeling frightened. Every time he thrust his spade into the ground he couldn't help but feel that there was someone - or something - standing right behind him, watching him. But each time he stopped and turned round, of course, there was nothing there.

Apart from the sound the breeze made in the grass there was silence everywhere, and he decided it was the silence that was really frightening him. "I'm sorry, but I have to do this," he said out loud as he thrust the spade into the ground with extra force and grunted as he did so, not just because of the effort but also to drown out any other sounds he might hear.

He wondered if he really did need to do this after all, and thought perhaps it would be better to leave the grass where it was and keep coming back every week to cut it down. Then again, if he didn't dig it up his mum might be cross, and he didn't want to annoy her.

By the time he'd carved out a lump of the grass his back was aching and his spade had actually bent. With a huge grunt he lifted the grass out of the ground on the spade, lowered it into the sack and dropped his spade on the ground.

He was just about to tie the top of the sack so that he could carry it more easily when something caught his eye. Down in the ground, in the hole he'd made by digging up the grass, there was something bright and shining. He bent down to pick it up.

It wasn't very big - it easily sat on the palm of his hand - but it was perfectly round and brilliantly white.

So brilliantly white that it seemed to be glowing from the inside rather than reflecting light from the outside. "Wow!" he said to it, "you're really pretty - my mum will like you!" and he popped it into his pocket to take home for her.

Then he tried to pick up the sack.

"Hurgh!" he grunted as he tried to lift it.

It didn't move.

"Huurrgghh!!" he tried again.

It still wouldn't move.

It was no good, he realised. It was too heavy to lift. He was going to have to drag it all the way home.

Five – home again eventually

The sack was so heavy that it took him a week to drag it home.

By the time he got back to the village he knew his mum would have used up all the food and money from his last trip. He couldn't sell this grass at the market, this lot had to be planted in the garden. And if it didn't grow they'd be in trouble.

His hands had been so tightly gripped around the top of the sack as he dragged it home that he could hardly open his fingers to let go of it. Instead of opening the front door he knocked on it with his head.

His mum was so pleased to see him she gave him the biggest hug he'd ever had. He stood on the doorstep gripping the sack as she smothered him with hugs and kisses.

"I was worried about you!" she said, "where've you been?"

"Dragging this thing! Give me a hand will you?"

"Don't bring it in the house!" she cried, "I've just tidied up. Come on, we'll take it round the back."

Together they dragged the sack to the back of the house and as soon as they were in the garden Sheng could see that his mum had been working just as hard as he had.

She'd borrowed two buckets and a long wooden pole from neighbours and she'd walked all the way to the lake with the pole across her shoulders and one bucket at each end of the pole. When she reached the lake she'd filled the buckets and then walked all the way back home again, slowly and carefully, so she didn't spill one precious drop of the water.

When she got home she'd watered the garden with the two buckets of water and then straight away she'd set off back to the lake for another two buckets,

then another two,

then another two,

then another two,

and so on.

She'd done this all day every day.

Five miles each way,

backwards and forwards

between their house and the lake,

so that by now it looked as if it might just work after all.

The garden was beginning to come back to life.

She'd even dug a hole ready for the grass to be planted in the middle of the garden. They watered the hole and watched the water soak into the ground. Gradually the water softened the ground and they carefully lowered the grass into the hole. When the grass was standing straight and proud they filled in the gap between the grass and the earth and carefully watered the grass itself.

Then they said a little prayer to the gods asking them to let the grass grow, because if it didn't grow

they didn't know what they'd do. All they had left to eat by now was enough rice for their next two meals - supper and breakfast. If it didn't grow they wouldn't have any food at all.

After they'd had a bowl of rice for supper Sheng was almost too tired to take himself off to bed. "Oh, wait a minute," he said as he got up, "I found this. I thought you might like it." He took the little round white thing from his pocket and gave it to her.

"Good heavens!" she said. "Where on earth did you get this?"

"It was in the ground when I dug up the grass," he shrugged. "It must have been there all the time."

"How strange," she said as she looked at it, "fancy finding one of these in the ground. People usually look after them better than that."

"Why?" he asked, "what is it?"

"It's a pearl," she said. "They grow in oysters in the sea, and when people find them they usually look after them because they're rather valuable." She looked up at him and smiled. "Well done! Not only is this beautiful, it could come in very useful next time we're really hard up because we can get a good price for it!"

"But if it's so valuable how come I found it in the ground?" he asked.

"I don't know," she said and then she laughed as she remembered something. "My grandad once told me dragons used to keep a pearl tucked in the folds of skin under their neck. Perhaps a dragon dropped this one and that's how you found it in the ground!"

"You don't believe that, do you?" he asked.

"Probably not," she laughed, "but stranger things have happened in the world."

"Yes, but dragons?" he asked, "you don't believe in dragons, do you?"

"Well let's think, my dad once told me that he had a friend when he was a boy whose grandad knew someone who says he saw one once when he was a small boy and he said what happened was -"

"I'm sorry mum, I'm so tired I have to go to bed," he interrupted her. "See you in the morning." He kissed her on the cheek and staggered to his bedroom. He didn't want to be rude, but he really didn't have the energy to listen to one of her long, rambling stories from when she was a girl.

She sat for a moment, holding the pearl up to the firelight. She'd never owned anything so pretty in her life, she thought, and it would be a shame to have to part with it. "I'll need to keep this somewhere safe," she said to herself as she looked around the room. She didn't have a jewellery box because she didn't have any jewelry. "Oh, I'm too tired to think about this now," she said. "I'll put it in the rice jar for the moment and find a better place in the morning." She dropped the pearl into the jar with what was left of the rice, put it back on the shelf and went to bed.

Sheng slept like a log and would have slept all the next day as well, but his mum came into his room in the morning. "Sheng," she spoke softly as she gently shook him, "Sheng, wake up! Let's go see how the grass is growing!"

He struggled with his clothes and staggered out to where his mum was waiting for him. She opened the back door and they stepped out together into the garden.

The grass was gone.

Overnight it had dried up

and crumpled to dust.

All that was left was a little pile of yellow dust in the middle of the garden.

His heart sank as he looked at it and thought of the long journey home,

dragging the grass all that way for nothing.

Nothing.

It had all been for nothing.

"There you are!" he pointed to the yellow dust. "I told you it wouldn't work!' he sat down on the ground rather sulkily. "Now I'm going to have to spend the rest of my life trekking backwards and forwards between here and where that grass grows!"

"Not the rest of your life," she tried to reassure him, "the drought will come to an end sooner or later and things will get better again. At least we know where we can get grass to sell."

"But we haven't got any food! What am I going to eat?"

"We've got a little bit of rice left for you to have some breakfast and I've got one penny to buy some more with for the journey. That'll have to do, I'm afraid."

"What will you do?"

"Don't worry about me," she said, "I'll find something."

By now they were back in the kitchen. Sheng sat glumly at the table with his elbows on the table and his head on his hands. His eyes followed his mum as she went over to the shelves and reached up. "That's odd," she said almost to herself, as she picked up the rice jar.

"What is?" he asked.

"The jar. It seems heavier than I - **WAH!!!!!!**" she yelped in shock as she took off the lid and looked inside.

"What is it?" he asked. She didn't reply. She stared at the jar for a second and then looked at him. Then she looked as if she was going to say something but changed her mind. She looked again at the jar and then turned to look at him. She took a breath and said "Did...." but then stopped and looked at the jar again as if she couldn't understand what she was looking at.

She looked up at him and said "Did you -" but that was as far as she got.

"What is it?" He asked. She was acting so strangely

she was beginning to frighten him.

"Did you fill this jar up last night?" she asked.

"No. I went to bed before you did, remember?"

"You didn't get up again?"

"I'd still be asleep now if you hadn't woken me up. What is it? What's the matter?"

"When we went to bed last night this jar was nearly empty," she said.

"There's still enough for breakfast, isn't there?"

"I reckon so!" she laughed as tipped the jar up over a bowl on the table and the bowl filled up with rice. As the last of the rice came out of the jar the pearl fell out and landed on top.

Sheng stared at the rice in the bowl and then burst out laughing. "Brilliant!" he said. "How did you do that?"

"I didn't do anything," she said.

"So where did all the rice come from?" he asked.

"I don't know," she said, "but I think it must be something to do with the pearl."

"How do you mean?" he asked.

"Well let's think this through," she said. "You found a patch of grass that was the only thing growing for miles around."

"Yes."

"You cut some down and brought it home, then went back for more."

"Yes."

"And when you went back for more you found the stuff you'd cut down had already grown back."

"Yes," he nodded.

"And when you went back again and dug up some of the grass you found the pearl."

"Yes."

"So the pearl was most likely under the grass all the time."

"Yes."

"But... when we planted the grass in the garden we didn't put the pearl underneath it. And the next morning the same grass was dead as firewood."

"But you put the pearl in the rice jar..." he could see where this was leading.

"And the rice jar is full!" she finished the sentence for him. "So I think the pearl must be magic. It was the pearl that made the grass grow and now it's made the rice grow."

"So if we put it back in the rice jar we can have free rice every day!" he laughed.

"I've got a better idea: we've got one penny left in the money jar. Let's put the pearl in the jar with the penny and see if it can make money grow!" They laughed with delight as she brought down a small jar from the very top shelf and took the lid off it. She dropped the pearl in, put the lid back on it and kissed it for luck before placing it back on the shelf.

In the morning they went straight to the kitchen and as soon as she picked up the money jar Xiang knew something had happened. She took the lid off and screamed in delight and amazement.

"What is it?" asked Sheng.

"Look at this!" she said as she tipped the jar up and

emptied the contents onto the table. Twenty golden shining coins fell out onto the table, spinning around and rolling towards the edge before Sheng caught them. Twenty gold coins! One gold coin would be enough to last them for a couple of years - this was all the money they would ever need in their lives!

They laughed and cried with delight as they counted them again and again and then made little piles of coins - five piles of four, ten of two, four of five and then two of ten - to make absolutely certain how much was there.

Twenty gold coins.

Enough money for the rest of their lives.

When they'd calmed down a little they sat quietly, staring at the shining, beautiful coins.

Twenty of them, arranged neatly in a square in front of them.

They would never be poor again.

They would never be hungry again.

Sheng would never have to go out to the desert again.

They would never have to borrow anything again.

They would never need to beg again.

Sheng would never again have to cry himself to sleep with hunger.

"You know what I think we ought to do?" he said after a while.

"What?" his mum asked.

"Shopping!" he shouted with delight and started to scoop up the coins but his mum reached out and

held his hand. "Wait a minute," she said, "let's not be hasty."

"But there's so much we could buy - "

"Yes, but wait. Let's think about this: yes, this is a lot of money. If we're careful this is as much money as I'll need for the rest of my life, and it's probably all the money you'll ever need as well. But what if we go to the market and spend half of this in one day and then find that the pearl in the jar trick only works once? We'll have wasted an awful lot, and that would be stupid, wouldn't it?"

"I suppose so," he nodded his head.

"And another thing," she continued, "everybody in this village, everybody in the whole county, knows we're the poorest people for miles around."

"But we're not any more because -"

"No! Listen!" she interrupted him. "No-one else knows about this, and they mustn't find out. We have to pretend we're still poor, even though we know we're not."

"I don't understand," he said, "why?"

"What do they like doing more than anything else around here?" she asked.

He shrugged his shoulders.

"Gossiping!" She answered her own question. "You know what they're like, they always want to know what everyone else is up to. If we turn up at the market shelling out gold coins here, there and everywhere they'll know we've come into money and they'll all start gossiping about it. You know what happens to gossip: it spreads really quickly. If they all start gossiping the robbers will find out that we've got money, and if they know we've got money they'll be down here in a flash to take it all from us and we'll be poor again!"

"Oh, yes...." he realised his mum was right. "So what do we do?" he asked.

"What we need to do is hide nineteen of these coins somewhere safe and take just one of them to market. With one gold coin we'll be able to buy everything we need, even if it's not everything we want."

Xiang was right. It wasn't the most exciting thing to do with the gold, but it was the most sensible. The floor of their house was just the ground the house was built over, they couldn't afford floorboards. So they dug a hole in the earth in the corner of the front room and hid nineteen of the coins in a small sack. They put the sack in the hole and filled the rest up with earth, patted it down and covered it with a mat. No-one would notice. Anyone coming into the house might well walk right over it!

Then they went into the village and with one coin they bought lots of fruit and vegetables and meat, even though it was really expensive. Then they bought new clothes, some furniture, and a horse and cart to carry it all home, and when they got home they still had most of change left from the first coin.

But of course they'd paid for the food with a gold coin, and the man they bought the fruit and

vegetables from bit the coin to make sure it was real before giving them the change. As Sheng and Xiang carried the food away he held the gold coin up for his wife to see. "They're supposed to be the poorest people in the village," he said, "so how come they paid for all that food with this?"

"Well, well, well! I wonder where they got that from?" she said, and later in the morning she mentioned it to the butcher's wife.

"That's funny," said the butcher's wife, "they bought a load of meat from us this morning as well!"

"That's nothing!" someone else overheard and joined in the conversation. "I saw them not half an hour ago driving off with a horse and cart piled high with furniture. If they're poor I'd love to see what rich people get up to!"

And so the gossip started to spread, just as Xiang said it would.

And it spread quickly, far and wide.

Six – it was bound to happen....

The next morning they rushed downstairs and found another twenty gold coins in the money jar with the pearl and the penny. They hid these coins with the others and then put the pearl and the penny back in the money jar.

And the next morning there was another twenty.

The morning after that there was another twenty.

And the next morning another twenty.

And then another twenty

and another twenty

and another twenty

and another

and another

and another

and so on.

Every night they left the pearl and the penny in the money jar, and every morning there were twenty more gold coins in the jar.

After just a few weeks they had hundreds and hundreds of gold coins hidden under the doormat. They were now the richest people in the whole of the province. They were probably as rich as the emperor of China himself.

And all this time the gossip was spreading from one person to another, and from one village to another. It

was obvious to everyone that Xiang and Sheng were no longer poor: Sheng wasn't going off to find grass anymore and Xiang wasn't asking people if they had any odd jobs that needed doing. They were buying the best food for sale in the village, and Sheng had even started going to school.

Their sudden wealth was the most interesting thing that had happened for miles around in many a long year, and everyone had a different idea as to what had really happened.

Someone said Sheng's mum had an uncle who was staying with them and he was a magician. Every time he saw a fly or an insect in the house he just pointed a finger and **BLAM!** - a puff of smoke, a flash of light, and the creature turned into a gold coin.

Someone else said he'd seen the uncle turning a mouse into a sack of gold coins.

A neighbour said she'd seen Xiang digging a big hole in their garden and said she must have found a gold mine underneath their house.

One of the market traders had seen her carrying a pole with a bucket at either end and these buckets were full of gold coins she'd found at the bottom of the lake.

Someone else said it was Sheng who'd got the gold. He hadn't been away for all that time just to bring back grass - he'd been working with the robbers, stealing from people in other villages along the river. Of course that was really unfair because Sheng had never done a bad thing in his life, even when he and his mum were really, really poor. But that's what happens - gossip always turns nasty in the end.

Eventually, of course, the robbers heard the rumours. Two of them were at the market in another village. One of them was pointing his knife towards the butcher while the other was filling a sack with meat he had no intentions of paying for. The butcher plucked up the courage to challenge the robbers. "Why do you always steal from the poor?" he asked. The robbers laughed loudly and one of them explained "Well we have to steal from someone because we're robbers, that's what we do. But there's no-one rich around here so we have to steal from the poor - there's no-one else!"

"Well that shows how much you know, doesn't it?" the butcher replied and when the robbers asked what he meant he told them that Xiang and Sheng were now so rich that it was said that the Emperor himself had asked to borrow money from them.

They went back to the mountains and told their boss what they'd heard.

"Why are you telling me this?" he asked them.

"We thought you'd like to know," one of them said.

"I'm not interested in other people being rich," the boss told them. "I want to be rich!!!!!" They looked a bit confused. "You nincompoops!" he carried on. "What's the point of coming here and telling me a load of gossip? I don't want gossip, I want money! If they've got money I want it - and I want YOU to GET IT FOR ME!"

"Right, boss!"

So later that night, in the middle of the night, when

the whole village was silent and everyone was fast asleep, Sheng was suddenly woken up by the sound of his front door being kicked in.

Crash!!!!!

He leaped out of bed, rushed out of his bedroom and came face to face with the two robbers. One of them was big and broad and bald, the other was short and wiry like a terrier. "What do you think you're doing?" Sheng spoke boldly even though he was quite frightened. "Get out of our house!"

"Tell you what," said the big one, "we'll go when we've got what we came for."

"What?" Sheng asked.

"The money!" the big one spoke to Sheng as if he was a baby. "Give - us - the - money!"

"What money?" Sheng laughed, "we haven't got any money!"

"Yes you have," the little one piped up.

"Sorry mate, you've got the wrong house," said Sheng. "Everyone knows we're the poorest people in the village."

"No!" the big one said. "Everyone says you used to be the poorest people in the village but now you're the richest. So give us the money."

"Oh, that's just village gossip," said Sheng, "you don't want to listen to gossip!"

"Give us the money!" the big one repeated.

"We haven't got any!" Sheng said.

"If you haven't got any money," the little one asked as he looked around him, "how come you've got all this posh furniture?"

Sheng hesitated for a moment and then said "My grandad left it to us!"

"I think you're lying," the big one said.

"If you're so poor," the little one went on, "how come you're wearing silk pyjamas?"

Again Sheng hesitated. Then he had an idea. "Birthday present!" he smiled.

"Stop messing us about," the big one took a step closer to Sheng, "and tell us where the money is!"

"I told you! We haven't got any money!"

"I'm losing my patience," the big one said. "I'll give you one more chance." Again he spelled it out as if he was talking to a baby. "Tell - us - where - the - money - is!"

"I keep telling you! We haven't got -"

The big one slapped him across the face. He flew across the room and landed by the kitchen shelves. It hurt where he got hit and it hurt even more where he landed.

He watched as the robbers began to tear the house apart looking for the money. They started with the cushions, ripping them to shreds, and then they began breaking the furniture into pieces. Sheng could see that they were not going to leave until they'd found what they were looking for. Sooner or later they would lift up the mat and find the coins hidden underneath it.

Then he had an idea.

He was close enough to the shelves to be able to reach up to the money jar while they weren't looking. As soon as he picked it up he knew by how heavy it was that the pearl had done its magic again that night. Keeping his eyes on the robbers he put the jar down beside him, took the lid off and felt inside for the pearl. Because his pyjamas didn't have any pockets he popped the pearl under his tongue to keep it safe and then poured the twenty gold coins out onto the floor.

"Is this what you're looking for?" he called out to the robbers. They turned around and their eyes lit up with greed and surprise. This was more gold than they'd ever seen at one time, and far more than they'd expected to find in the house.

"Ah, look!" the big one said, "he's remembered where he put the money!"

"Good boy!" the little one said as he bent down to pick up the coins.

That was when Sheng made the mistake of saying "Just take the money and leave us alone, will you?" but he couldn't move his tongue because the pearl would have popped out so it sounded rather strange.

"What's the matter with your mouth?" the big one asked.

"Nothing," Sheng replied, but again it sounded strange.

"Yes there is," the big one said. "You're talking funny."

"No, I'm not."

"You got toothache or something?"

"No, I'm fine."

"Let's have a look," and with that he picked Sheng up by the throat and as he was lifted up Sheng accidentally swallowed the pearl.

GULP!

"Nah," the big one said as he opened Sheng's mouth and looked at his teeth. "They look all right to me," and he let go of Sheng, who fell back onto the floor. By now the little one had finished picking up the coins. "Thanks for the money, kid," he smiled at Sheng. "Now don't forget, if you get any more give it straight to us - it saves a lot of bother all round. Bye!"

And with that they skipped over the door they'd flattened and set off down the road towards the lake, laughing as they went.

Seven – every silver lining has a cloud...

Sheng sat perfectly still.

Something strange was happening to him.

He could feel the pearl in his throat.

Not because it was stuck - it was slowly slipping downwards - but it felt bigger than it should have done.

It also felt warm.

So warm that it seemed to be drying him up inside as it slid towards his stomach.

He remembered how thirsty he'd felt when he'd been walking to and from the desert and realised he was almost as thirsty as that now.

His mum tip-toed out from her bedroom and raised her eyebrows when she saw him. "It's all right," he said, "they've gone."

"I'm sorry," she said, "I shouldn't have left you to tackle them on your own but I was so frightened. Did they take everything?"

Sheng shook his head. "Only what was in the jar from tonight. I gave them that before they could find the rest of it."

"Clever boy!" she smiled, then she looked at him more closely. "Are you all right? You look a bit strange."

"I feel it," he nodded. "I got hit here, and it hurts,"

he pointed to his face, "and it hurts here where I landed." he pointed to his bottom. "And I've got some bad news: I'm afraid I've swallowed the pearl."

"Oh, don't worry about that," she said. "We've got more money than we know what to do with. But I am worried about you. You do look a bit strange, a bit.... green around the gills."

"Can you get me some water?" he asked. "I can feel the pearl going down my throat but it seems to be getting quite hot and it's making me thirsty." She scooped a bowl into a bucket of water from the lake and passed it to him.

He drank it down in one go and said "That's not enough, pass me some more, please." He slurped that one down as well and asked for another, and when he'd slurped that one down he said "Still not enough - can you pass me the bucket?"

GLUG!
GLUG!
GLUG!
GLUG!
GLUG!

He gulped all the water from the bucket in a few seconds and even that didn't make him feel any cooler.

But while he was drinking he had an idea.

He didn't understand how, but he suddenly knew that he needed to get to where this water had come from. He somehow knew that if he could get to the lake and swim in the water he'd be all right.

He put the empty bucket down and leaped up.

"I've got to get to the lake," he said. "I'll see you later," and then he ran out over what was left of the door.

Xiang ran out into the street after him. "Sheng!" she hissed down the road, not wanting to wake the neighbours. "Sheng! where are you going at this time of night? Sheng, come back!" It was no good, he was almost out of sight by now so she ran down the road after him.

She needn't have worried about waking the neighbours. The noise of the door being kicked in and the house being smashed up had woken most of them and they'd been peering through doors and windows, wondering what was going on. They guessed the robbers had come for the money, and some of them thought it served them both right for pretending they were still poor when the whole world knew they were rich.

When they saw the robbers laughing as they left the house they thought the excitement was over, but then they saw Sheng running after them.

Where's he going? Some of them wondered. Perhaps he was chasing the robbers to get the money back - this would be a punch-up worth seeing!

So as Xiang ran down the road after Sheng, half the village ran down the road after her.

There were no street lights in those days, of course, but the night was so bright with so many stars in the sky that they could easily see where they were going. They got to the lake just in time to see Sheng standing on a rock at the edge, and Xiang standing further back calling out to him.

"What are you doing?" she was shouting. "Have you gone completely mad? You can't even swim!"

"I'll just have to learn!" he called over his shoulder and dived into the water.

Splash!!!!!

GULP!
GULP!
GULP!
GULP!

He swallowed as much as he could and it did make him feel a little cooler.

Cooler, but not better.

There was something very strange happening to him, but he still couldn't work out what.

By now the pearl was in his stomach and felt as big as a melon,

but that wasn't the worst of it.

He was having pains.

Sharp, stabbing pains shooting right through his body, tensing muscles he didn't even know he had until now.

It was a beautiful, clear night. There must have been a million, trillion stars in the sky and the light from the stars was so bright that it was even lighting the lake underneath the surface. Sheng could see quite clearly under the water.

He suddenly noticed something else happening: his skin was changing colour!

His arms were turning greeny-blue and were covered in scales as if he was a fish. What on earth was going on?

Then his hands tightened up and turned a darker colour.

They were turning into claws.

His fingernails grew longer and longer and a moment later they were sharp talons!

Then he needed to take a breath.

He floated up to the surface of the lake
and took the biggest,
longest,
deepest
breath he'd ever taken in his life.

Hhhhhhhuuuuuuhhhhhh!!!!!

He didn't know his lungs could hold so much air.

Then he felt the need to stretch his arms and legs and as he did so he found himself lifting up from the surface of the lake into the air. He looked around to see what was happening and then he realised:

He'd
turned
into
a
dragon.

His mum had said he looked a bit 'green around the gills' after he'd swallowed the pearl, but he didn't realise how seriously she'd meant it.

Then he realised - of course! - his great grandfather was right! Dragons really did keep a pearl under the folds of skin at their neck, and what he'd found under the grass must have been a dragon's pearl.

That's why it had made the grass grow.

That's why it had made the rice grow

and the money grow.

And now he'd swallowed it the pearl had made him grow.......

into a dragon.

The people of the village stood still and watched in amazement as the first real dragon they'd ever seen rose out of the water and flew around the edge of the lake over their heads. Then, as it flew off towards the mountains on the far side of the lake it twisted slightly

to look back over its shoulder and let out an unearthly, howling, horrible screech, which was a dragon's way of saying "Bye, Mum, I'll see you later!"

As if all this wasn't strange enough they saw, as the dragon came up out of the lake, that the water on his wings and on his back didn't fall back into the lake as he flew away.

It gathered in mid-air to form a cloud - the first cloud they'd seen all year.

And they watched in amazement as the cloud floated gently back down the road towards the village.

When it was over the village it burst open and the most beautiful, soft, gentle, thirst-quenching rain pitter-pattered over everybody's garden and brought everything back to life overnight. By the morning the land had turned brown and fertile again, the fruit had grown back on the trees, the crops were growing once more in the fields, and the dried up riverbed was covered with deep, clear, blue flowing water.

It's said that dragons live for a thousand years and it must be true, because for the next thousand years that village didn't have another drought.

Even in the hottest, driest summers there was always that one little cloud hanging around, making sure everything was all right and nothing got too hot and dry again.

Meanwhile Sheng, who was now a dragon, had flown off towards the caves where most of the robbers were fast asleep.

The entrance to the caves was guarded by four robbers sitting around a bonfire.

They saw something out of the corners of their eyes
and when they turned
and saw what it was
they screamed in terror and ran away

one to the north
one to the east
one to the west
and one to the south.

They never came back to the caves in the mountains, and when they met other robbers they warned them not to go near the village, or the lake, or the mountains, because it was all guarded by a fierce dragon.

So for the next thousand years the people of Sheng's village weren't troubled by robbers. Every robber in China knew that village and its people were protected by a huge, fierce dragon.

And as for the other robbers, asleep in the caves, let's just say .....

there are different kinds of toast that a dragon
can have for breakfast!